'writer shelby c'
spelled this way, on purpose
RAPPER TAKE BACK CREW

my movie idea, has an, all black cast, 'rapper take back crew',
here's the characters, and there handles
my wife 'killer d' or 'kd' her real names 'kd'
my handle - 'main', but my real name 'writer shelby c'
                and our rap band is called 'take back crew' or
'tbc'
'aj's wife' sam
'jj's wife' sara
buddy #1 - 'aj'
buddy #2 - 'jj'
jj and aj, are brothers, they finally got married
'eli', aka jackboy, he's a hustler trafficker, long time buddy,
and jacker of drugs
'luda' thats his name, he's a big time drug broker, and jacker
of drugs
feret #1 - 'lightning' he's the guy, he's super quick
feret #2 - 'duce' she always gets it done, on the second try
'they're both specially trained, for special missions, where
size matters'
my guy rottweiler - 'thug' he's trained, 'thug, get in your cage'
my girl rottweiler - 'texas' she's trained, 'texas, get in your
cage'
'they're specially trained, for different mission'
our parrot - 'biker' cause 'he used to be owned by a biker, so
he talks, biker talk'
and our guard cat - 'claws' he actually guards our house,
where we all live
'he's called claws because he, claws on the back of your
ankles', 'he's saying hi'

'we have a 'big red, lexa, panic button', at the end of the
kitchen counter, and he
'hops up and pushes it, when local guys, come around, he's
smart', 'he'll hit the jack button'
our moto - 'we'll, get it back'

im shelby c., but my handle's 'main'
people alway go
'happenin, main'
'whered, you go, main'
'puff, puff, give, main'
'sup, main'
we alway sing, 'we love rippin, rippin, rippin'
and 'look, we ripped anutha crook'
thats why, 'we drippin, drippin, drippin', main
'yes, im an actual rapper'
i was born in may 1972, at the end of the vietnam war, by
1982, when i was 10, 'rap', became a big deal, and by 1983
when i was 11, i was already singin, break dancin, writing
rhymes, and rappin. then in 1985, when i was 13, we moved
to south l.a., supriseingly i fit right in, before you know it, i was
hangin, slangin, and lightly bangin, i became, 'a boy, from the
hood'. i soon met two of my closest friends in the world, we
were better than brutha's, because we were tite with each
other, and protected each other, stood up, for each other.
there's 'mutha' which stands for m.f.'er, but his real name is jj,
we're the same age, and his one year, older brother 'playa',
which is short for player, he can't keep it in his pants, there's
a string of girls, that follow him around.

by 15, we were talking, marine corp,, and by 16 years old, we
were planning on joining it, all three of us joined at the same
time, and signed up for 4 years each, it was 1989, i was 17, i
also married my girl 'kd', right before we left, it was a small

affair, just some buddies and some 'money, down, the drain',
anyway, us boys left that summer. luckily, we all got back
right before christmas 1993, 3 ex marines, on the war path,
man, the bar life and hustlin, was made for us, we coulda
moved anywhere, but we decided to stay in the l.a. area, so
we got a nice place, over by the airport and helicopter
companies, me and jj were 21 and aj was 22. the first thing
we did, was start up a rap band, we called ourselves 'take
back crew', and we started doing shows all over the
southwest and l.a.,

we always play our 'bigtime base, mega triple platinum, songs
and hits', ha, like,
'shelby's song, the girls, they role in
'shelby's song, dope star's
'shelby's song, dope anthem
'shelby's song, cartel
'shelby's song, the devil, went down to downey
'shelby's song, drunken roper, theme song
these are actual songs, you can hear, summer of 2020, to
begin with

boy was it fun, girls galore, 'we damn near broke our sock,
tryin to do a, ho, a day'
thats how, we got our name out. it wasn't too long before our
business line rang, the business line is my phone, and no one
calls me, since im married to 'k', but i alway yell, 'kd', answer
that. she said, 'a rich girl lost her phone', and i said, 'rich girl
huh, what up', then 'kd' bumped me, and i said, 'knock it off',
the rich girl said what, and i said, 'not you', then she went on
to say, 'im only here, visiting, my sister, in college', she said,
'im from mexico, im very wealthy, and a thief took my phone,
it has all my banking information on it, and pictures of me
naked', then she said, 'it had to be one of the six people, who

were there', and i said, 'ok, well how much do i get paid', and
she said, '1 million, if you get it back in the next 3 weeks', and
i said, 'my two buddies, are getting married, in exactly 3
weeks, atleast i won't forget the deadline', but then i said, '1.5
million, so that all 3 of us get, $500,000 each' and she said,
'deal, here's the information', and i told her, your welcome to
put other crews on it too, to try and get it back, and she said, 'i
have, and your the 2nd crew, so if you see them, just say,
we're the 2nd crew', and i said, 'ok', at first we had no idea,
what we should do first, and we had three weeks, and she
gave us $300,000 to start with, and we get to keep it,
regardless of our search results.

so, we did what we alway do, we all went to the bar, to
discuss things, then, one thing led to another, and by the end
of the nite, we had a plan. a computer program, to tell us
when her phone is actually being looked at, a place to stay for
a few days, thats near our targets, and 6 drones, that we'll
launch, at one time, and all 6 of there cameras, will be
monitored, at the same time, from all of our laptops, actually, i
like android. anyway, 3 drunken ex marines, really tore that
bar up, we pulled down the chicken wire, and the band kept
playing, with beer bottles and cans, going everywhere, i
always pray for perfect luck, and perfect timing, and on this
one, we got out of there, just ahead of the dirty pigs. we
assumed this girl was ligit, she couldn't have been older than
21, if she was a villin, she musta started out, when she was a
kid villin, but her moneys good. so we rented a big three
bedroom place at 'business suites', we got it, for the 3 day
weekend, we had to nail down, wich one of these fools, stole
her god, damn, phone, you know what we say, 'we'll, get it
back'. we were a little hung over, so we told the 'girls' politely
to 'beat it', then we all grabbed our 'drone bags', each bag
has one drone, and its support gear, then we laid them all out,

on the floor of the suite, then we turned them on, made sure
that they worked, and then we sinked, them all up, to our
computers, and made sure the camera's were good, i
personally, charged all our batteries, so power, shouldn't be a
problem. then we sinked up our watches for some reason,
we each had two people to spie on, so we looked at our
computer program, it said that someone was looking at the
phone, so we launched, all 6 drones, luckily, all 6 fools lived,
not far from our victims house, so we all worked together,
smoke in mean green, laughin, and tellin jokes, while we
spied on them, for some reason, her phone's gps doesn't
work, she's probably a thug, i said. well, it didn't take long, for
us to find the culprit, a short, balding man, he looked mexican,
so i yelled, 'essay' has it fools, then jj and aj said, 'knock it off,
main', then we all double checked his address, and hit auto
return, on all 6 drones, and they flew right back to where we
launched them, in the 'business suites' parking lot, i tore my
gum in half, and marked where my two took off, and sure
enough, they came right back, and landed exactly on the
gum, neat, we spy'd during the early evening, so they couldn't
see our drones, now back to the bar, we're supposed to meet
back up with kristi, and these super hot, twin chicks, the bar,
is where, brilliance is made, thats where, we do our best
thinking. as our drone was leaving, we noticed a security sign
in his front yard, so by the end of the nite, we decided to have
nancy lee, make us some security uniforms, and signs, for the
side of our stolen work rig. the next day, i flew my drone
super high, over his house, and we waited for them to

leave, when they did leave, which was around noon, we ran
straight over there, walked up to the front door, and i shorted
out the security system, while jj and aj were walking around
the house, looking for broken windows, they told the
neighbors that there was a silent alarm, that tripped, and that

the police are on there way, then i quickly ran in, grabbed her
phone, from where i watched him hide it, then i came back
out, i winked at jj, so he would call my phone, when he did,
my phone rang, and i pretended to be talking to my
superviser, 'uh huh, uh huh, false alarm guys', so we told the
neighbor's 'please call us, and the police, if you see, anything,
suspicous, ok' and they all said, 'ok'. so we took off, nice and
slow, like we hate our job. then, on the way home, we met up
with the girls at the grocery store, because we're having a big
bbq, we were all staring at her phone, and i said, its all locked
up, i don't know how he got it to open up, and then i said, 'its,
not very, bling'd up, for a girl, then everybody said, throw it, in
the car and lock it, so i did, everyone even watched me, but
when we came out, our car had been, 'broken into', so i
looked inside it and said, they only took some dvd's and some
weed, then i kept looking, and said, 'and they took the phone',
we all screamed 'mf'er', then we all laughed and said, 'atleast,
we have the $100,000 each, and we still have 2 weeks left, so
we carried on, and looked at the stores camera's, from home,
aj, the older brother, is a computer freak, and player, so he
started to look for clues, the first clue was, that i forgot to lock
the drivers door, and after a couple hours, of looking at the
tapes, still nuthin, back to scare one, and now the phone is
off.
then they all started giggling and singing, 'if you got a million,
five, don't, send, main, main'

i was a little depressed, so i went lookin for a lowrider, to buy,
just to go get beer, and clown around, so i looked around, and
found a blue 83' regal, i said, do you have the stock rims, and
he said, ya, so i looked at it, it had a high rise, hood, a
corvette engine, and badass 15inch speakers, he said the
only thing wrong with it, was that the 'heater fan', wasn't

working, he wanted $25,000 firm, so i just kept staring at it,
and was petting some little weiner dog puppy's,
then i said, you can keep the tuner, i just want the amps and
speakers, and he said cool, and then he quickly pulled the
tuner out, then i said, i have a weiner dog at home, his name
is 'hercules', and i'll give you full price, if you throw in 2
puppies, he said deal, i payed him, and at home, me and 'k'
named them, 'fritz and frita', now 'hercules' has buddies to
play with, i already have to big dogs, 'thug and texas', so we
hope, they'll get along. the next day, i went down to the local
stereo shop, and picked up a 'hide', that fits exactly 2 keys,
you just tilt up the whole dash pad, on top, well, it didn't take
long to install it, you just pump the brakes twice, and turn the
ignition key, to augzilary power, and it automatically pops
open, but then i realized, that everyone does that, and it kept
popping open, so switched it to, 'push on the breaks, then hit
the cruise control button, then the dash pad, flips up, and
open', it works great, it works perfect.
later that day, jj and aj, stopped by to check out my new hide,
and i was trying to figure out why the fan motor, kept coming
on, but, the air wasn't blowing, so i grabbed the wrench, and
popped the fan off, man, it had the motor, but the fan was
chopped back, and there was a dusty 'key', so i tasted it,
pretty good stuff, almost pure, i would classify it 'un cut', and
since we're in l.a., i would value it at a solid 36 grand, what do
i alway say, 'the devils, on my side', so i said, 'thank you
devil', i owe you one, they laughed, and said, 'im grabbin
some beers, and i said, 'your going to buy beer', anyway, it
was neat, how it fit, perfectly inside, so i said, 'blow, brutha's',
and we all dug in, we started laughing, drinking beer, and
doing 'blowcane', then i cranked up, some of our new music,
its called, 'hood country', songs called,
'dead warden', and
'ho lean', along with, many others,

people love our music, and reader's, it's 'real', these are real
songs, 'check them out, 'google them' under, 'take back
crew', or 'writer shelby c'
then, we started relaxing, and we all agreed, with the car
costing 25k and the blow, being worth 36k, i made a healthy
11k profit, and i got a really fast, plain jane, get away car, with
no navigation or gps tracking, just leave your cell at home,
and get away with.

just when i was really feeling good, and gettin super faded,
my phone rang, and it was my 'x', from a long time ago, we
dated for along time, she told me about one of our old
enemies, 'dude', ripped her car, but i call him 'dud', she said
he's the one, and 'she got it all on tape and i saw it for myself,
so theres, no regrets' it was 'her favorite hit gun', 'a model
1911, '45' old faithful', she says, 'its the only thing, thats been
faithful, to her, in her whole life', she counts on it, now people
are screamin what, 'yes, she does hits, on the side', 'yes, she
makes extra cash on the side', her names, 'haley', but we call
her 'heat', cause, she's alway packin heat. why a '45', 'cause,
size matters', then i said, 'well even if you miss em, the noise,
will scare em, to death, main'. i figered i could handle this
one myself, so i told the boys that im going to go jack 'dud',
and get her piece back, then they said, 'we're comin, we want
to watch', and i said, 'grab a slurpy fools, and stay outa my
way, this fool, just direspected heat', then i thought to myself,
'i really want this fool gone, so i told everybody, that he's,
'he's, the leak', then we saw him at a light, and i bailed out,
ran over, and hopped in the back of his car, and screamed,
'keep drivin, dud', wheres her fn piece, he said, 'here', and he
pulled it out of his britches, and right when i was going to
make him leak, a sherrif pulled up next to us, at the light, so
said to dud, 'this aint over, its the beginning', and i bailed out
of dud's car, and hopped in aj's, they said, 'tough break, with

that police pulling up', and we all laughed, then we gave
'heat', her favorite gun back, i got a free bj out of it too, look at
me now.

i really needed to take a week off to clear my head, but it
never works out like that, one of our border guard buddies
called us in a panic, 'come over come over', 'sheila', is
holding the 'pay off list', for 'ransom money' , she wants, 'a
cool million, in twenty's', then i said, 'we better hurry, before
she screws up l.a.'s coke supply', then jj was talking to him on
the phone, and kept saying 'uh huh, uh huh, then ok', so i said
'what now', and jj said, 'on social media, she driving your
white range rover, main', i said, 'what', so we drove by the
house, and sure enough, 'this crazy ditch, ripped, burgled,and
jacked, our whole house, not just the rover', i said, 'i think we
all concur, that crazy ditch, is going down, then aj said, 'i
second the motion', then i said, 'the motion carrys', lets get
er'. so we went back to the bar, to come up with a plan, then
we went back to the house, so i could log onto my computer,
then i turned on 'auto tracker', typed in my plate number, and
bing, she's in central l.a., heading south towards the 'hustle
casino', then we geared up, and i said, 'lets ride, did you bring
the 'auto kill', and aj said ya, you just point it at the engine
compartment, and it tells the car computer to shut down, just
like its out of gas, it really works great, i bought it off a guy
from 'mother russia', for 3 grand, he can even get you a
stolen plane. we were behind her, when she turned into the
casino, we were right behind her, so we honked and yelled, hi
bitch, then she stabbed out, but there was no place to go, so
she drove right thru the plate glass window, and started
driving thru the casino, right past all the slots, we followed
close behind in my other vehicle, the 'ta ho', people were
freekin, people were yellin, and people were winnin, and
cheerin, us, then she drove thru, the other plate glass, hit a

concrete flower planter, and popped my new tire, 'i couldn't get a clean shot at it, with the auto kill, cause she was, driving so crazy', then we rushed the car, pulled her out, dis armed her, coughed her to a hand rail, then we jacked the 'pay off list', out of her purse, took her drugs, then we took her money too, for the tire, $200, then we hopped back in my ride, and took off, exiting the casino, just, as the pigs, came role in, in, 10 deep, they popped her for grand theft. then we made it home and told our buddy, to stop by the house, and pick up the list, cause we were bbq'n, and drinkin, about 2 hours later he showed up, and man was he pissed at her, we said, here you go, then he gave us 10 grand each, and 50 grand for my ride, cause, thats what it took, to get the list back, then i said, she might have taken a picture of it with her phone, i said, half a unit for her phone, and i tossed her phone to him, then he ran to his trunk, came back, and he said, 'your lucky, last one', then we partied down, we were all complaining, what a monday, 'we need a break, man man man'.

the next morning, right after 'k' went to work, i checked my fantasy football on 'the outlaw's and thugs league', a league that i personally invented, it will be real one day, we don't care if you got cases pending, we here to play ball, i imagine a player being arrested for a triple murder, right on the field, before half time, because the warrant, finally went thru, and players doing coke and drinking whiskey at half time, 'we don't drug test', take steroids and play ball, they say we're a bad influence on the 'kids', but we don't care what the kids say, so play ball', everyone, tunes in, to watch us play, broken arms, goujed out eye's, missing teeth, detectives lurking around, 'the other league's, are sissy league's', 'compared to 'the outlaws and thugs football league'.

$then the phone rang, its was an important 'blow broker' out of 'tj', i call him 'gus', and his wife ivon decarlo, tall hair, they're very nice people, she's so sexy, i refer to his wife as 'full blown', 'tj and full blown', because of the her hair. his specialty is smuggling by 2inch pipeline, but he does well as a broker too, he has 10 big houses with basements, thats where they have a machine that mixes 25% uncut coke, with 75% clean, purified water, otherwise it would turn the coke yellow, anyway, they dig a tunnel, the install atleast 3 pipelines, so that when one plugs up, they just use the other ones, then they fill the ends of the tunnels in, just the ends, so there no evidense of a tunnel, then they back a full 53 footer up in mexico, pump it across, one truck per day, the machine on the american side, 'use centrifical force' like the spin cyle on the wash, then they have a metal conveyor belt that takes the damp coke thru a propane or natural gas dryer, it comes out at the end, where they squish it back into keys, and then tape and package it. if you put there coke, next to normal coke, you can tell the difference, try it, it works great', anyway he has 10 houses that i know of, so it must be 10 fully loaded 53 footers per day', i say, 'thats respectable', but you have to think bigger, much bigger, like maxed out c17's and edwards afb too, also, both at the same time, feel me. anyway there's just 3 pipes sticking up, and the tunnels half filled in, and they're not going to dig it out, 'so the us, won't ever know, where the source is', neat huh. tbc has smuggling idea's too, but we won't get into that now, well i will say this, 'how about 36 drones, each carrying 1 full key, flying across the border fence, and dropping all 36 in the back of your dually pickup, the beds illuminated so the drone pilot can see, the only way to stop a drone, is to crash another one into it, and the us won't do that, so it works great, just wait till all 36 drones drop, then drive off, its easy easy, peezy'. then it heads north east. that can work for places where there's a 4 or 5 story building, all 36 guys can stand on the roof, to fly them, 'its hard to stop a swarm, do it when there's no moon'

so i said, hold on, let me conference call it, with aj and jj, they said, 'como esta, cavrone, and he said, 'primo, i need favor, i'll pay you good, just get my rv back, it has 8 thousand pounds of blow, stacked up, in the back', we said, what happened, and 'jose' said, as soon as i got the new 'pay off list' for the american border guards, he goes, 'i payed them the 100k into there account, but as soon as we were just past 'el centro', we got pulled over, and the guards jacked the load', we said, holy moly, we goin up against the guards again, we figured they hid the new rv in the dessert somewhere, so we called pete, our helicopter pilot, and we went looking for it, it shouldn't be hard to find, since it has 'jose' painted on the roof, in big red letters, so the mexican bandits, won't get him, when he's leaving mexico, they shoot from cliffs, and block the winding roads, in the hills, of old mexico. so off to the airport we go, he said he already deposited a cool mil. in our account, since we worked for him before, sure enough, it was there, 'he musta new, we couldn't refuse', after a few hour, on the way home, we saw it, and called 'jose', it was parked close to the airport, where we took off, the irony, anyway 6 black tahoes rushed the place, right as we were landing, even though they got it back themselves, we still got, our second mil., it pays, to stay sharp, then we figured we'll go to vegas for a few days, just the boys, so we did.

we got into vegas, late at nite, after the l.a. bars closed, like 4:39am, man, were we drunk, a limo driver named 'lyle', was standing there as we exited the plane, he took us out the private, 'star exit', down to the lower part of the airport, and we quickly jumped into the limo, before we drove off, we all

did a fat line, on the back of his clip borad, then we said, 'lets
check in, at the 'gold digger, motel', next to the strip, so we
did, then lyle said, 'where we goin', and i said, lets get some
take out, now, put it in the truck, then we'll go 'ho hoppin',
thats where you go from strip club to strip club, we start at a
club thats not have bad, then, we work our way down to the
'scuzziest, strip clubs', man, is it, the right thing to do, anyway
we had fun, met some 'skinny chicks', and went out drinkin,
before you know it, we were at there motel, 'spades', and we
ended up making a home, made porno, look it up, its called,
'cunning clone girls 3', we got flat rate for our time, but we
hear, 'its selling, well', anyway, we made it back to south
central, by saturday at noon, just in time to bbq and drink
some beer, i finally looked in my bank account, a cool 13 mil.,
and i reminded aj and jj, to answer there phones, when our
girl accountant calls, because we pay our taxes every quater,
that way, everything stays ligit, we launder the money thru
several ligit business's that we own, the smartest thing the
three of us did, was 'to buy half of a small casino in nevada',
we just drop off the millions, and they deposit the laundered
money into our accounts, we also do 'security consulting on
intellectual property', we can charge alot, for that.

we got back saturday morning, and by noon, we were bbq'ing,
we had half a pig, and all of our friends, then some long time
friends stopped by, we hadn't seen them in awhile, our
friend's 'eli' aka 'jackboy' and 'luda', both stopped by, but they
had a strange look on there face, they're usually, the life of
the party, then they pulled me inside my house, and i said
'whats up', i said,
'let me shut the sliding glass door', then,'biker', our parrot,
started talking biker trash, 'spec, get me a beer', 'spec, steal
some dope', 'spec, lick my bike clean', 'spec, lay, my, wife,
now, so she'll, leave, me, alone'', then 'claws' our guard cat,

wouldn't leave us alone, we couldn't even talk, meow meow, he kept rubbing on the 'red panic button', that came with my 'lexa', he was meowing, as to say, 'is everything cool, or are we being rushed', so i said, 'claws', everythings cool, get down. then i said, jackboy, where's, yo mask', and eli went, 'ha ha, it aint me foo', he said that, 'the corner crew', and 'ten hides', snatched up 'luda's girl', me, jj, and aj, went, 'what', and luda said, 'somethin, somethin, 100 billion dollar deal, a 53 footer, full with uncut, cane', our jaws dropped, i accidentally, snorted, most of my blow out, then looked up, and said, 'good lick'.

then we started talking in depth about the situation, he said, 'they've had her for a few hours now, and they're keeping her for insurance, 'against the 'jack' 'the rip off'', i said, 'we can't do nothin till nite, so lets take a few minutes to, get a plan together, i said, they'll expect us to sneak around the back, but instead, we'll just kick in the front door, they won't be expecting that, then we'll just grab 'hailey', she's the one, we call, 'heat', cause she always packs. they all agreed, 'the five of us, against a mexico's. top drug broker', then we told people that we were going to the store, to keep up the apearance that we didn't know about it yet, so hopefully, they won't be waiting for us. i was already half drunk, from partying all morning, so as we left, i grabbed 'my two attack ferets', 'lightning and duce', and i was playing with them as we drove, i was in the back of the tahoe, sitting inbetween 'luda and eli', as we roled, they kept bitching 'keep them off me keep them off me, damn', so i said 'get off me, get off me, damn'. according to our calculations, this should be a piece of cake, just go over and kick the door open, like the marines, then i crossed my fingers for good luck, and looked up, and jj said, knock it off, so i said, knock it off.

we new the approximate area, so we headed that way, as we drove, we hacked 'cali trans', found out his plate number, looked up his address, there's rumor's, that he has an automatic, machine gun, security system, with like, 13 machine guns, but we're not worried, they won't slow down, a freight train', i knew i shouldn't have brought our two rottweilers, 'thug and texas', but we walk them to get intel, right before we go in, and i don't know why i brought our two ferets, 'lightning and duce', i think i brought them cause i was high and drunk, but regardless, it all worked out, except lightning kept chasing duce back and forth on the dash, then the dogs wouldn't stop barking, i politely yelled at them to 'shut the f up, now, or no dog food for you', i swear, they understood every word, by the look on there faces, we were getting close, so we rewinded all the traffic tapes, to find the location of the second house, his stash house, it worked like clockwork, we rolled up, hopped out, ran up, and kicked in the front door, but she wasn't there, and the maid said that she was at the other house, 'we had the maid call him, and tell him that thugs broke in and ripped off his house, she talked him into coming over to look at the damage, thats when we drove to the stash house, saw the bodyguard and her, in the downstair's of the hillside house, what to do, what to do, what to do, we ended up sitting there for about 2 minutes, before i came up with a great plan, it just came to me, 'lets burn them out' so i hopped out, popped open the back of the tahoe, told the animals to stay, then i grabbed the 2 cans of gas, that i previously filled for my dirt bikes, then i said, follow me.

we just started spreading gas, we were pouring it, over the three sides of the house where they couldn't see us, that when i clinched my right fist and said, stop, gun, gun, gun, just to point them out, to everyone, then i lit it up, the whole house was on fire, the guard came running out the front door,

but aj knocked him out, with one punch, then we ran arounds
back, bashed out all the back windows of the house, we were
just starting to pull 'heat' out, when i saw this little 'bemji' type
dog, bouncing up and down, in the next room, i looked thru
the window, and he was trying to push a big red button on the
wall, i yelled hay the dog is trying to activate the guns, the
guns were pointed right at us, and guided by motion
detectors, so eli, ran into the other room, and grabbed the
little dog, that was a close one, at least three machine guns
were trained on my junk, ooh, we were out of there in less
than ten minutes, and the guy, only saw 'aj', so the rest of us
can go to the drug transaction, without being confronted by
them, no sweat. now, on to phase two, getting away with the
whole 53 footer, so we went back home to come up with a
plan, then i noticed, we stole, fools dog. then we had to stop
by the store, on the way home, but we made it back to the
party, in less than, an hour, people at the party said, your
back, where'd you get the little dog, then i said, i don't
remember.

we ended up getting 'heat' back, saving the day, burning
dudes house, played with the dogs, and made it back to the
party in time to get lit and do my share of the killer cane. 'one
perfect day'
we called the 'tj outfit', and they were good with us still, so
they let the transaction go forward, they just said, 'open up a
swiss bank account, it costs like 20 bucks, we said, ok and we
started up an account and buy something, to verify, that it
works, so i ordered a 'perc', off the dark web for 10 bucks and
it worked, it should be here, next day air, then, they just said,
'be at the warehouse we use, on monday morning at 7am, so
we went, we were there about 5 minutes early, the timing was
perfect, we went in, shook hands with the 'essays', then the
guys from 'the corner crew' and '10 hides', showed up, there

were 3 trucks backed up to the warehouse, from left to right, a 53 footer of pallets of beer, then a 53 footer of un cut cane, our load, then an empty 53 footer, but the warehouse door on the far left was closed, so they only saw the two trailers, anyway, they transferred money to the 'essay's account and our account', then the mexicans told them, make sure and grab the truck on the left, then aj, the guy they saw, he drove away with the truck on the far right, so when they hopped in, they drove off, with the truck load of beer, not the cane, as soon as they left, we promptly hopped in the cane truck and took off, to split it with the 'essay's', since they were in on it, it worked out great, we got our 5 billion and half a load, and the mexicans got there, 100 billion and half a load, 'straight legendary',

 as we were leaving the 'essays's' warehouse in east l.a.,, my phone rang, it was them, the mexicans, they said, can you help us out again, we need a hand, and i said, probably, stop by our house saturday around 9 am, so they did, we were already lit from watching 'the outlaw and thug football league', the 'l.a. thugs' were playing the atlanta 'dirty birds', what a good game, l.a. 'won', and we didn't talk business, until after the game was over, 'man, they got class, them essay's', we said, 'whats going on', they said, 'a rougue coast guard outfit, called 'alfa 1' out of 'diego', they've been planting evidense and, 'jackin, dope, daily', they keep 'f'n with the supply chain, and interupting the big loads, i told them, 'until we get a grip, on the boat crew, the dipatch, and the heelow crew, 'deliver by water, only at nite', they already knew, but they said, thanks, the 'tj's', want there stuff back, and they want us to deliver a message to them, 'if they cross them again, they will all disappear', we said, 'got it' and started thinking of a way, to get the 'cg's', 'to bring the product to us', straight doin it, the easy way, 'my way', 'if we think it out, it should be a piece of cake', the devil's on our side.

then we asked the 'essay's', 'do you have any 'dirt' on the 'cg's, and they said, just on there 'boss', 'rear admiral weakcannon', i said, 'good, then they'll bring it to us, we just have to call him, and meet up with him, its a piece of cake, no sweat', the essay's said, its half a 53 footer, so they'll have to return it, in 2 of the big, moving trucks, and i said, i'll, tell him'. apparently, the mexicans set him up, by providing 3 hookers, free drinks, big cash, and free blow, and it return, he lets occasional big loads thru, the admirals been on the take for a while, the only catch, is that the mexicans recorded the entire thing, on digital spy cam, the minute the admiral put the straw to his nose and snorted, that minute, they had him, they got him, the next day we met up with him at a local motel, called 'the hood arms', we showed him the video, passed the death message, and then we told him, what he was going to do, we had a gun to his head, and we had him call them guys and set up an immediate meeting, it musta went good, because the next day he said that he had the 2 trucks ready, and we instructed him, to go to our friends house, out by the airport, we met up and the 'essay's had 8 regular vans, right there, in a perfect line, ready to be loaded, it went perfect, and they gave us their assurance, that if they see a boat, 'with the mexican flag, painted on the side', they are to totally ignore it, and leave it alone, then we doubled there 'pay off money', things went perfect.

well 2 days till the wedding, so i started especially training the 2 ferets for, suicide missions, flying drones by remote control, and to bark, when someones coming, and i time them, on there escape, from a targets house, they have to get out of there quick sometimes, espially when they pull a gun, we let

them drink beer, but they only, lick on the blow, usually, only on the weekends.
i still can't believe that aj and jj, are marrying exact twins, same hair and everything, two light skinned girls, they used to be actor's, but they didn't get paid enough, so now they role with us, when it comes to guarding our old craftsman house, in old town l.a., they guard it, just as good as 'thug and texas', come on dogs, kennel up, then texas started chasing the neighbors cat, so i yelled, 'texas, get in your cage', meanwhile aj and jj, 'mulled over, how to launder over 5 billion dollars', thats not easy, sometimes, i said, 'don't forget to, use the currency detergent, with no bleach', we all laughed, then we thought to ourselves, 'the congress are straight pro's, at getting away with, laundering big time money', so we just called our congress woman, from southern california, so cal., ca., cali., she called us right back, and we set up a meeting at the roler rink, and we talked as we skated, what a blast, we even 'did some cain, in the back of her big black car, main', none of us remembered, what we agreed to, but, the money just started flowing, we each had a special, 'trust card', and we started spending freely, she laundered it so good, that we ended up on the cover of 'fordes' magazine, and we made the top 200 list, but think its cause of how popular we are too, 'success alway shine, on ex marines, i swear', we each got 1.2 billion on our trust card, so 3.6 total, 3.6 billion out of 5 billion total, we keep it in a big houston bank, thats run by crooked guys that launder mexican drug money for congress, she told us wich bank to go to, then ask for the assistant manger, and quietly wisper, 'tj's toys', he treated us like gold, main. 'i guess we own the leading, genetics outfit, anyway it pays, in spades, 'thanks management', thats what i call, 'who ever's running earth, from far far away', its possible,

the morning of the wedding, and 'sam and sara' are looking
pretty, as usual, the girls had the idea to marry the dogs and
ferets too, 'so we're marrying, thug and texas, and lightning
and duce', a bunch of people said they're going to film it, then
we looked for the booze, we stashed it on the side of the
church, where people get ready, but apparently, the girls hid
it, so we had to 'go get more', then they jinxed us, 'be safe', i
just shook my head, kd won't say that to me, since 'everything
we do, is dangerous, you dig, my man'. anyway we pulled
into 'hood liquor' and grabbed what we needed, some dude
grumbed 'penguin', so i grumbled, 'we feel, sorry for your
mutha', then he took a few pots shot at us, as we were
leaving, so we promptly chased him, there were two cop cars
sitting right there, but l.a.'s finest, didn't do nothin, we musta
chased em foe a mile, then they dove there car into a strip
club parking lot, 'we all, took a big swig, and dove in after him,
we cut off a cop that time, but again, he did nothing, so we
chased 'fool', 'into the club and beat him down, right infront of
the cats, at the cat's house', thats where the pussy is, but we
safely made it back in time, 'you thought we were gonna get
arrested and miss the wedding, huh', 'we made it', here
comes lightning and duce, there feret tukseedo's and
everything, here comes thug and texas, there doggy
tukseedo's, they snortin and walkin proud, boy, camera bulbs
flashing, for the black and white photo's, digital recorders
recording hopefully, and here comes the sam and sara, then
the grooms, aj and jj, they all made a half circle, 'then they all
did there vows, 'we could barely hear lightning and duces
wedding vows, but we could hear thug and texas's wedding
vows, very clearly'. it was a quick ceremony, 'the girls did it
that way, so that, the guys wouldn't have time to back out, im
sure', eli and his girl were there along with his granny and 3
brother's, 'luda' he was there with his girl and her parents
showed up, the rear admiral, weekcannon, was there with his

wife, we're all buddies, and that 'crazy, sc, mean shot caller', he was there with his girl 'k', and she had 9 of her friends with her, so it was sc and 10 girls, he calls it, 'a ten ho', we were singing, and everybody had a great time, time to party, at the reception.

anyway, as they left, kd said, 'the dumpsters right there, im fin to, clean the trash outa the tahoe, and i said, wait wait, there might be good stuff mixed in, and sure enough, i found the girls phone, from our first job, it was in a jack in the crack bag, 'good golly, molly', so i called her, then me and kd went over to get our reward, as soon as we handed her the phone, she said, 'hold on, let me transfer 500 million, from my ex boyfriends account, to my swiss account, i said, we just got a swiss account too, how did you verify it, she said, 'on the dark web, i bought 10 valumes for ten buck, i said, 'no way, i bought a perc for 10 bucks', then kd bumped me, and the chick giggled, she goes, 'i already gave you 300 thousand right, so i owe you you guys 1.2 mil. still, i said 'ya', she said, whats your account, so i gave her the swiss account, not the 'tj's toys' account, and she goes, 'well, im done, i transfered 8 mil., and i said, 'thats perfect', call us anytime, and kd bumped me again, i said, i can't wait to tell the boys, once they get back from there honey moon, in monty carlo, they'll only be gone for a few days, then they're coming right back, and we're all going to paris and london for a month, 'the good life'
thanks god!
then we ran into, an old adversary, 'spooky', he had another lie and another idle threat,
we've got peoples stuff back, 3 times, from him

mean ole dealer
huntin on, numba '1''

take back crew, and the devil,
were just
 havin, fun

thank you, everyone
the end,
get the three dots, 'the crazy life', main
copyrighted7683words
2020